# Diamonds and Earls

Caroline Johnson

Diamonds and Earls
Text Copyright © 2016 by
Caroline Johnson

ISBN-13:
978-1540652607

All rights reserved. This book or any portion thereof may not be reproduced or used in any manner whatsoever without the express written permission of the publisher except for the use of brief quotations in a book review.

This book is a work of fiction. Names, characters, places and incidents are either the product of the author's imagination or are used fictionally. Any resemblance to actual persons, living or dead, or to actual events or locales is entirely coincidental.

First printing, 2016

Publisher
Love Light Faith, LLC
400 NW 7th Avenue, Unit 825
Fort Lauderdale, FL 33302
www.LoveLightFaith.com

# DEDICATION

Dad, thanks for always being there.

# CONTENTS

Chapter 1…pg 1

Chapter 2…pg 11

Chapter 3…pg 20

Chapter 4…pg 31

Chapter 5…pg 44

Chapter 6…pg 58

Chapter 7…pg 75

# Chapter 1
## THE GIFT OF FRIENDSHIP

When a woman nears the day of her wedding, she often finds herself without sense or caution. Much was the same for Lady Henrietta Boyle, who was so delighted with her circumstances that she was unaware of any strife or struggle that might be happening around her.

"Lord Pembrooke," she said, smiling as wide as can be, "I am quite delighted about this dinner this evening. How wonderful it will be to enjoy some time with our friends before our wedding."

Henrietta was a tall, slender woman with wide blue eyes and hair the color of straw in the middle of a summer's afternoon. She stood beside her brother, Lord Boyle, with the very same hair color, but eyes the color of clovers.

"It is quite hard to believe our wedding is in less than a fortnight," a dapper gentleman replied. Unlike his betrothed, The Earl of Pembrooke's hair was as dark as night, slightly curly, and he had eyes the color of stormy clouds. He reached for Henrietta's hand and squeezed it. "I wish that it was tomorrow, if I could be so honest."

"I do too, darling," Henrietta replied.

Lord Boyle rolled his eyes dramatically. "Now, now, you two. Let us ensure you reserve your passionate exchanges for the wedding, shall we?"

The couple smiled at each other and then laughed.

"So let's see these fabled jewels you have told me so much about," Lord Boyle stated.

Lord Pembrooke smiled and turned to the cabinet set into the wall behind him. They stood in a smaller sitting room at the back of the house where the warmest afternoon sun reached, full of comfortable armchairs and bookshelves stacked high with more books than one could ever count, and a place that Henrietta greatly looked forward to spending time in when she and Lord Pembrooke were married.

The cabinet looked inconspicuous, made of a beautiful polished walnut, yet as Lord Pembrooke opened it wide, Henrietta had to stifle a gasp at the sparkling gems that were revealed when he stood aside.

Even her brother, Lord Boyle, seemed rather impressed.

"My heavens, I have seen nothing quite like this in the whole of my life," he said, smiling at Lord Pembrooke.

"Indeed," said Lord Pembrooke. He grinned at his bride-to-be, and said, "What do you think, my love? Can you imagine yourself wearing such fine jewels on the day we are wed?"

Henrietta took a tentative step towards the cabinet, and peered more closely at the jewels.

There was a beautiful set of gems; a necklace made of five large diamonds, the middle stone larger than the rest, nestled in gold settings with a matching ring of considerable size, surrounded entirely by tiny emeralds.

The way the sunlight shone on them, they appeared to be glowing as if they were tiny stars in the dark cabinet. She longed to reach out and touch them, and at the same time, feared that they were far too priceless to be held.

"Dear sister, you will be as ravishing as a princess in these stones," her brother said, patting her on the shoulder.

Henrietta beamed. "I don't know about that…"

"Nonsense," agreed Lord Pembrooke, nodding to Lord Boyle. "I am certain that there has never been a princess alive who has been, or who will be, as beautiful as you will be."

There was a knock on the door, and Lord Pembrooke said, "Come in," in response.

The door pushed open, and Lord Pembrooke's butler, Mr. Hughes, stepped inside, bowing his head. "My Lord, your guests have arrived."

Lord Pembrooke and Lady Henrietta smiled at each other.

"Thank you, Mr. Hughes. We will join them shortly in the drawing room."

Mr. Hughes smiled, his bushy mustache tilting up at the corners, and excused himself from the room.

"My dear Lady Henrietta, I have a request for you," Lord Pembrooke said, looking down at her. "I wondered what your thoughts might be to show your jewels to our friends this evening?"

Henrietta furrowed her brow. "Why do you need my permission?"

Lord Pembrooke shrugged his shoulders. "You will be the one to wear them, and I don't wish to spoil the surprise if you wish to keep it as such."

"I think it would be wonderful for our friends to share in our joy," she replied. "I am certain they will feel just as in awe of them as we are."

Lord Boyle nodded. "I think they will greatly appreciate seeing them, for they are quite priceless pieces of your family's treasure."

There was another knock on the door.

"Mr. Hughes, I told you that we would join you all momentarily."

The door opened, and the three turned to look to see who had come in.

Another young man with dark hair, slightly shorter than his older brother's, strolled in the room. His high cheekbones and gentle eyes scanned the three standing beside the cabinet.

"Oh, it's only you, William," Lord Pembrooke said, turning to close the cabinet to the jewelry, looking relieved. "I wondered if perhaps Mr. Hughes had decided to be his typical assertive self."

"Nonsense, brother," said Lord William, smiling at them all. "Ah, Lord Boyle, and Lady Henrietta. How wonderful it is to see you once more."

"A pleasure," Lord Boyle replied, nodding his head and shaking his hand. "How have you been, friend?"

"Quite well, quite well. Attempting to avoid my brother in his fierce preparations for this wedding that is so quickly approaching."

"Not fast enough, if you ask me," replied his brother, grinning. "Shall we join our friends in the drawing room?"

"Indeed we should. They are all waiting anxiously to see you," replied Lord William.

The four of them made their way from the room, and Lord William hung back to stroll beside Lady Henrietta.

"How are you feeling, Lady Henrietta? Still certain you wish to marry my brother?" He asked, winking at her.

Henrietta laughed. "Oh, Lord William, your

games always amuse me so. I do hope that one of my children will inherit your wit and charm."

"Do you not think that my brother is charming? Perhaps we should keep that between you and me." He laughed, and she joined in.

They stepped into the sitting room and were greeted by the faces of their friends. At once, Henrietta approached the beautiful Lady Charlotte, who had been Henrietta's closest friend growing up. She embraced Henrietta tightly.

"Oh, dear cousin, how glad I am to see you!" She cried, pulling away from her, beaming. "It has been far too long."

"Hasn't it only been a week?" Henrietta replied, laughing.

"Still, far too long!" Lady Charlotte said in response.

There was another face that appeared beside her cousin's, with thick mahogany hair and piercing silvery blue eyes, a broad smile on her bright red lips. Henrietta's face lit up.

Henrietta embraced the new woman as well. "Oh, Lady Mary! I am so pleased that you are here."

Lady Mary hugged her tightly in reply. "I would not miss this dinner for the world!" She answered, still smiling.

Henrietta looked back and forth between her two

friends. "I truly cannot share with you how grateful I am that you have come to help me prepare."

"What good are friends if we are not helpful as well as beautiful?" Lady Mary replied, fluttering her eyes and brushing a hand over her lovely hair.

Lady Charlotte and Henrietta laughed.

"Darling, let's not forget our other guests," she heard Lord Pembrooke say to her, not unkindly. He smiled at her. "We will have plenty of time to catch up with everyone."

"Of course," Henrietta replied, smiling at her betrothed.

She turned to see a couple sitting upon the settee, a lovely pair that Henrietta recognized at once. She curtsied to them. "My Lord and Lady Wingfield. How wonderful it is that you could join us this evening."

"Dear Lady Henrietta, we are most pleased to be able to!" Lord Wingfield replied. "It has been far too long since the ball at Frostfield Park, and we are so honored to be able to join you for your wedding and all of the festivities prior."

"Thank you so much for thinking so highly of us to invite you to your celebratory dinner this evening," Lady Wingfield said, her voice quiet and smooth.

Henrietta beamed at the pair of them. "We would never think of leaving you out!" She took a step closer to them and said, "Truly you both are some of the few whose company we truly find enjoyable." She turned to look up at Lord Pembrooke, who was speaking with the other couple on the other side of the room. "I was overjoyed when he suggested a dinner with our closest friends to celebrate our marriage before the big ceremony."

"It is just an excuse to have a social gathering," Lord Wingfield replied, smiling at Lord Pembrooke's back, and his wife tittered. "Your betrothed would throw a ball in celebration for his great uncle's, niece's, uncle's, brother's, son's newest born child."

Henrietta laughed out loud.

"Darling, Lady Wilds just shared something with me that you will be most interested in," Lord Pembrooke said, gently touching Henrietta on the shoulder.

She smiled at Lord and Lady Wingfield before turning to the other couple.

Newly married, Lord and Lady Wilds stood beside the window, held hands and gazed lovingly into each other's eyes.

"Good afternoon, Lady Henrietta," the man with a tall stature and a brightly-colored kerchief said, his bushy brows and pointed nose smiling at her.

"Good afternoon, Lord and Lady Wilds," she answered. "Thank you so much for coming to our little dinner."

"We have been so looking forward to this evening," Lady Wilds said. "Your future husband and my husband would never miss an opportunity to get together and act like schoolboys once more."

Henrietta smiled.

"Tell Lady Henrietta what you were telling me, Lady Wilds."

Lady Wilds smiled up at them. "Well, we would like to offer you a wedding gift," she paused, looking straight at Henrietta, "A fine stallion. We just inherited one of my father's horses; the offspring from a strong and wild beast that he used for breeding. We believe he will be a great racehorse."

"Your horse has won many races recently. Is that correct, Lord Wilds?" Lord Pembrooke asked, his hands behind his back, an eyebrow arched.

Lord Wilds nodded his head. "Indeed. We spoke about it and agreed that it would be great fun to attend a race together and watch as our horses, or their offspring, compete against one another, wouldn't you agree?"

Henrietta smiled as she watched her betrothed's face in response. "Why, that's a marvelous idea. You are far too kind, dear friends. We are very grateful for your generous gift."

"Think nothing of it," Lord Wilds replied. "I believed that you would be happy with such a gift."

"Have I seen the horse you are gifting us at your stable?" Lord Pembrooke asked.

"I am unsure if you have seen it, but it is the chestnut Thoroughbred."

"That beautiful creature? You wish to part with it?" Lord Pembrooke questioned.

Lord Wilds nodded his head. "I am happy to do so, for such a friend."

There was some rustling beside the door, and they turned to see Mr. Hughes reappear in the door, a smile beneath his bushy mustache.

"Dinner is served, my Lord."

## Chapter 2
## TRUTH OF AN ARRANGEMENT

After dinner, the party retired to the sitting room at the back of the house. They had enjoyed a lavish dinner with many toasts to the happy couple, and there had been much laughter and jovial conversation.

"Friends, friends!" Lord Pembrooke said, tapping the side of his glass. The room grew quiet, and they all looked up at him and Henrietta, who stood beside him. "We are so happy that you came to visit us. We are so looking forward to our wedding, and we are so thankful that you have all agreed to come and witness our marriage."

There were murmurs of agreement from everyone, and smiles from all around the room.

"We also would like to share something very special with you," Lord Pembrooke said. "My family has a very special wedding tradition that has been observed for the last few generations, and we are keeping that tradition alive with our wedding."

He turned from them to the cabinet they had been looking at earlier, and he swung the doors open, revealing the jewelry.

The guests all got up and surrounded the tiny cabinet, gazing down at the jewels.

"Lord Pembrooke, where did your family come by these jewels? I have not seen their equal," Lord Wingfield said.

It was Lord Pembrooke's brother, Lord William, who answered, rather assuredly. "Our grandfather, the Duke of Hallington, was given these precious jewels from a member of the royal family, his cousin in fact."

Lord Pembrooke nodded his head, and continued where his brother had left off, "He had done some great service for the royal family, and been given the jewels for his wife as a sincere thank you. He passed it onto my father, who allowed my mother to use it in their wedding ceremony, and now they have given us permission to use it in ours."

"That's simply wonderful," Lady Mary said.

"They are absolutely stunning!" Lady Charlotte said, smiling up at Henrietta. "What a beautiful bride you will make."

"The most beautiful," Lady Mary agreed, beaming at her friend.

"Such rare and precious jewels," said Lord Wilds. "They are truly a splendid family heirloom." He smiled down at them, as he stood nearly a head taller than Lord Pembrooke. "Thank you for sharing these with us, friend."

"Certainly," Lord Pembrooke said, ensuring the cabinet was closed tightly. "We are just so very excited for the wedding, and we cannot wait for the day to arrive."

"You won't have to wait long now," said Lord William, smiling at Henrietta.

She smiled at him in return. Her heart was warmed by all the love that she felt from everyone in the room. She felt incredibly blessed to have such wonderful friends and family who were as excited for them as they were for themselves.

As they settled back down into their seats, Lord Wilds spoke up. "So you have been betrothed for many years now, have you not?"

Lord Pembrooke nodded his head in response. "We have. Since I was nearly ten years old and she was…what…six?"

Henrietta nodded her head. "I was six, wasn't I? It feels as if I have known I was to marry you for my entire life."

"Do you remember when your parents told you?" Lady Wilds asked, getting comfortable for what she assumed was going to be a story.

"We were together, actually," Henrietta began,

looking over at Lord Pembrooke, smiling. "Your family had come to visit mine at our country home, and our parents had been in discussion all day. Not that any of us children noticed; we were far too busy playing in that wide, field behind our home."

"If I remember correctly, it had snowed the night before, right?" Lord Pembrooke added.

"I don't think it had, brother," Lord William chimed in. "I think it snowed the following night."

Lord Pembrooke shook his head. "No matter," he replied, still smiling. "What I do remember is that we had spent a great amount of time outdoors, and our parents had called us inside, just the two of us, and left our siblings outside to play."

Henrietta nodded. "My mother was the first to speak, knowing that it would probably startle me."

"She had said, 'Children, we have something very important to discuss with you. Something that you won't quite understand, but we believe it will be the very best thing for you.'" Lord Pembrooke said.

"And I remember just looking at one another, confused," Henrietta said, laughing. "She went on to say that as a group they had all come to this decision, and that while we may not like it now, one day, we would be happy with it."

Lord Pembrooke looked at Henrietta, and suddenly, the two of them felt as if they were simply talking to one another, and that they were entirely alone in the room together. He smiled tenderly at her. "My father took over the conversation, and told us very plainly that they had decided they we were to be married when Lady Henrietta turned twenty-one years of age. The union would benefit both of our families, and ensure both of us would be taken care of and have a comfortable home."

"Not that we understood what most of that meant," Henrietta added, brushing the hem of her dress smooth. "We were far more concerned with being able to return to playing with our friends and siblings. To us, the future was far away, not something to be concerned with. How quickly it surprised us."

Lord Pembrooke added, "And now, looking back on it, I couldn't have been more pleased with our parents' choice. There was no need to spend night upon night at social events, pretending to laugh at jokes that were not amusing, making flatteries that meant nothing, and dancing with those who we had no desire for."

"So you are both pleased that you didn't have to seek out your own mate?" Lady Charlotte asked, studying her friends.

"Absolutely," Henrietta said. "I agree wholeheartedly with Lord Pembrooke. All of the confusion, heartache and frustration have been removed for us. We were able to spend our time together getting to know one another before our wedding. It has been quite an amusing experience."

"So did you often think of the fact that you were engaged? When you were young?" Lady Mary asked.

Henrietta shrugged her shoulders. "I probably thought of it more frequently than he did, since most young ladies often dream of love and marriage when they are young. And as I said, it certainly was quite the relief to know that my husband was to be a person that I already knew and found to be quite amiable."

Lord Pembrooke raised an eyebrow. "Quite amiable? Is that how you perceived me as a child?"

"There are many things that I could have perceived you as; be grateful that I was as generous as I was! If only I had known what sort of man you would become!" Henrietta replied, a playful tone in her voice.

Lord Pembrooke smiled wide, his smile softening Henrietta's heart. The rest of their guests laughed, and the whole night felt as if it were out of a story. Henrietta's heart was full, and she longed for the evening to last forever. There was nothing more precious to her than the company of her friends, and to have them all in the same place felt like a dream she had long cherished had come true.

Lady Wilds stifled a yawn, and with a sinking heart, Henrietta smiled at her friend. "We do not wish to keep you any later than you can stay, dear friends."

Lady Wilds' eyes grew wide, and she waved a hand in the air, dismissing Henrietta's words. "Oh, do not worry about me, Lady Henrietta. The journey today simply seemed to have been more tiring than I had anticipated."

Lord William got to his feet and nodded at his brother. "It is getting late, brother. We should allow our guests to retire for the evening. We will have plenty of time together this week."

Lord Pembrooke nodded his head, setting his goblet down on the ornately carved table beside him. "Of course. We do not wish for you to feel as if you have to tarry here; we would not be the friends we claim to be if you faint of tiredness because you stayed at our expense." He bowed his head to the group. "It has been an absolutely brilliant evening, and we are both so glad that you are here to help us celebrate our wedding."

The group all gathered their belongings and said their goodbyes, which turned into more conversations, embracing and well wishing. Eventually, when the moon was high in the sky, the Wilds and the Wingfields called for their carriages to take them to the Inn in town where they would stay for the short time left before the wedding.

Henrietta and Lord Pembrooke waved as their carriages disappeared down the long drive, and shortly after returned indoors where their remaining guests waited.

Lady Charlotte and Lady Mary smiled at Henrietta from inside the doorway, and they found Lord William and Lord Boyle conversing beside the door to the drawing room.

"What a lovely dinner party," Lady Mary said, her eyes glimmering in the lamplight.

Lady Charlotte nodded, clasping her hands together. "There are few greater pleasures in this life than spending an evening such as this one with friends such as we have."

Henrietta smiled. "I couldn't agree more."

"We should retire for the evening," Lord Pembrooke said to the group. "Tomorrow will come early, and I must admit my weariness."

"Good idea, brother," Lord William said. "A good night's rest would do the future bride well," he said, winking once more at Henrietta, who laughed in reply.

Lord Pembrooke embraced Henrietta, and only released his hold on her when his brother cleared his throat rather loudly. Henrietta's brother laughed.

"All right, come now, you have a marriage to prepare for!" Lord William said, grasping his brother's arm. "My apologies, Lady Henrietta. My brother is such a passionate man."

Lord Pembrooke smiled at her. "All right, good night ladies. I do hope you all sleep well."

"Thank you," Henrietta said, smiling up into his face. "You as well, my love."

"And thank you for allowing us to stay here as well, Lord Pembrooke," Lady Charlotte added, inclining her head.

"Yes!" agreed Lady Mary. "You are most kind, my Lord."

"Think nothing of it; I knew how much help you would be to my betrothed in this busy time. I am glad you are here."

The group retired to their rooms, Lord Pembrooke and his brother to their individual rooms,

Lord Boyle to a guest room, and Henrietta, Lady Charlotte, and Lady Mary to a guest suite prepared for her by the Marquess and Marchioness of Crettingham, Lord Pembrooke's parents. The night ended quietly, with nothing to trouble them but a chittering owl outside, bathed in the light of the moon.

## Chapter 3
## THE DIAMONDS OF PEMBROOKE PLACE

The next week passed quickly, and the wedding date was only one week away. Henrietta and Lord Pembrooke had welcomed many guests in that time, and Pembrooke Place was full of joy and anticipation.

Lord Pembrooke and Lady Henrietta found themselves once more in the sitting room at the back of the manor, the warm afternoon sun glinting off of every shining surface in the room. The couple was sorting various gifts that they had been given, attempting to arrange them in such a way that would still allow the room to be used. Lord Boyle, Henrietta's brother, hovered near the window, watching the festivities with a look of amusement on his handsome face.

"Never in my life did I imagine I would receive quite so many gifts for getting married!" Henrietta said, examining a beautifully carved crystal bowl. "Surely people know we would have been happy simply by their presence at the ceremony."

"Giving gifts is a way for people to demonstrate their affection for the bride and groom," Lord Pembrooke said. "Are you unhappy with the gifts?"

"Of course not!" Henrietta said, startled by his words. "Do not mistake my shock for dissatisfaction. I am simply humbled by such generosity."

"Honestly, sister, you'd think that no one had given you a gift before in your life," her brother piped up, taking a few steps toward them to inspect the dish for himself.

Lord Pembrooke smiled at his fiancé. "You are quite beautiful when you are flustered."

Her face flushed, and she shot him a teasing glance.

The door to the room opened, and Lord Crettingham stepped inside the room, bringing an air of regality with him as he always did. He was a shorter man than his eldest son, with thick white hair and a wide, bristly mustache. His eyes, however, were bright blue and kind, and he wore thin spectacles. He smiled at those in the room before closing the door behind himself.

Lady Henrietta immediately rose to her feet and bowed to him.

"Dear girl, you mustn't insist on doing that," Lord Crettingham said, crossing the room to her. He gently placed a hand on her shoulder. "A week from now we will be family, and you must promise me that you will treat me as such."

"Yes, my Lord," she replied, and resumed her seat in front of the gifts.

"My, such lavish furnishings," Lord Crettingham said, smiling down at their collection of new items. "These must be the most beautiful things that you have received yet."

Lord Pembrooke agreed, but Henrietta glanced behind her at the cabinet. "My Lord, I still believe the gift that you have given me is by far the most precious," and she gestured to the closed doors. "I look forward to wearing them."

"So the Lady is pleased with the jewels?" Lord Crettingham said, moving across the room towards the cabinet.

Henrietta nodded vigorously.

"Good," he said, smiling.

Lord Pembrooke rose and crossed to the cabinet as well.

Not wishing to miss another chance to see the beautiful jewels again, Henrietta made her way to stand beside her fiancé.

"Can't quite get enough of them, can you?" Lord Crettingham teased, his hands on the doors. "I understand; they certainly are something to behold."

And then he pulled the doors open, a wide smile still on his face, his bristly white mustache turned up at the corners.

She heard Lord Pembrooke emit a gasp of disbelief.

Lord Crettingham, hearing it as well, quickly turned his gaze toward his son. "What is it?"

Henrietta watched as Lord Pembrooke pointed, his eyes wide, down at the empty cabinet.

Empty.

"But they were just there!" Henrietta exclaimed, her stomach feeling as if it had dropped to the floor. "Weren't they? Just the other day!"

Lord Pembrooke's face had drained of all color, and the only sound he could produce was something akin to a stammer.

"What is the meaning of this?" Lord Crettingham questioned, turning to his eldest son. His brow furrowed and his mustache quivered. "Where are the jewels, Daniel?"

Henrietta felt a twinge of fear.

"Just as Lady Henrietta said," he replied, stepping closer to the cabinet. He bent down and looked up inside of it, and up and down all sides, as if perhaps they had simply become stuck on the walls of the cabinet instead of laying nicely inside as they had done. "This is where I had left them."

Lord Crettingham sighed heavily, brushing his hair flat with his hand.

"Now is not the time for panic," Lord Pembrooke said, turning towards the others.

"Do you have an idea where they might be?" Lord Boyle asked, approaching the cabinet.

Lord Pembrooke swallowed, and began to speak. "There have been many people in and out of this house, and I must admit that many days in the last week are blurring into one. I do know, however, that I would never have moved them from here."

"But perhaps someone else has?" Lord Boyle replied, glancing at his sister.

"I have not seen them since the night Lord Pembrooke showed them to me!" she replied indignantly.

"Nor have I," replied her brother.

"There is no sense in allowing ourselves to run away with our fear. Let us be wise and first look for them. I am sure it is just a simple misunderstanding. I am not doubting you, son," Lord Crettingham said, noting his son's sallow face. "You have been preparing for a wedding, and I have not met a man who is able to maintain complete composure before he is wed. There are far too many important things for him to think on."

His son smiled gratefully at him, but Henrietta could still see his reservation.

So began the grand search for the family's inherited, precious diamonds, and it consumed the greater part of their day. They began in the sitting room where the jewels had resided. They checked each cabinet, pulled every book from their shelves, and looked beneath every piece of furniture.

Soon after they had begun, the news had traveled through the house that part of the bride's wedding attire had gone missing, and the door to the sitting room, standing open, was visited by many. Lady Mary and Lady Charlotte shortly joined them in the search.

When they felt they had thoroughly searched through the sitting room, they spread out to other rooms in the manor. It was the first time that Henrietta regretted the fact that her future home was as large as it was; how were they ever to find the jewelry in a place as large as this?

Lady Mary and Lady Charlotte followed her into the dining room, which was furnished with a long cherry table with enough chairs to seat a few dozen guests; a large, golden gilded mirror; and a long line of family portraits.

Henrietta sighed heavily. "Of course the jewels are not in here. Why would anyone have brought them in here and forgotten about them?"

Lady Mary patted her arm affectionately. "Come now, dear. We won't know unless we search."

"We understand your distress, cousin," Lady Charlotte added, nodding her head. "We will find them. I truly believe it."

The ladies began their search at once, pulling open drawers, checking beneath chairs, lifting tea sets and candelabras.

Henrietta noticed that Lord William had joined them, and she found herself grateful for more help in their search.

"Lord William," she said desperately, crossing the room to him. She clasped her hands together beneath her chin, and looked up into his face beseechingly. "Have you seen the diamonds that I am to wear at the wedding?"

Lord William tilted his head to the side, studying her face, clearly bewildered. Then recognition of what her words must mean dawned on his handsome face, and his eyes grew wide. "Whatever do you mean?" he asked, as if he did not wish to know the answer.

She quickly explained the situation, surprised that he had not yet heard of it. The whole house appeared to be in a tizzy. "Do you have any idea what could have become of them?"

He leaned against the doorway to the room, crossing his arms over his chest. His eyes searched the floor, "I'm afraid I do not," he replied, sadness obvious in his eyes. "I am so very sorry."

How very much he looked like his brother, she noticed, not for the first time. The same shape of the chin, the same width of his jaw, and the same shape of the eyes.

Henrietta sighed, looking over her shoulder at the other girls who were looking at them, expectantly. She shook her head, and both of their shoulders slumped ever so slightly.

"I would be quite happy to help you look,

however," Lord William added hastily. "If you so wish it."

"That would be wonderful," she said, "But perhaps you could be of more use to your brother."

"Oh," Lord William replied. "Right, of course. Where might I find him?"

"I believe that he and your father were checking the foyer, wondering if the jewels had become mixed up in some of the boxes to go to the chapel the day after tomorrow."

Lord William smiled and nodded. "Don't worry, Lady Henrietta. We will find those jewels. On my word."

She smiled as he excused himself from the room.

When night fell, and they felt as if they had thoroughly exhausted all of the possible places the jewels could be, they reconvened in the sitting room.

Lord Boyle, Henrietta, and Lady Mary entered first, with Lady Charlotte following soon after. Lord William, Lord Pembrooke, and their father entered last.

"So no one found the jewels?" Lord Crettingham said, attempting to keep his voice calm.

No one said a word in reply. The tension in the room was nearly palpable, and Henrietta was not keen on the look on her fiancé's face.

"Did you question all of the staff?" Lord Crettingham asked Lord Pembrooke.

He nodded in reply, and said, "Not a one had

seen them. Most were unaware of the fact that we even had the diamonds in the house."

"What on earth could have happened..." Lord Crettingham said.

Lord Pembrooke shifted uncomfortably.

"Something must have happened since you saw the jewels last. When was the last time you saw them?"

Lord Pembrooke glanced briefly at Henrietta before replying, "Saturday evening, I believe."

Lord Crettingham turned to face him, a peculiar look on his face. "Last...Saturday? You mean the night that you had your dinner party?"

"Yes."

Lord Crettingham stroked his mustache with one hand, his eyes glaring into his son's. "Did you, by any chance, share the location of the diamonds with your guests?"

Lord Pembrooke, his hands clasped tightly behind his back, lost some of the color in his face. He stared back at his father, his jaw tight. "I did."

"You did?" his father replied, his voice growing louder, his brow furrowed. "Do you have no sense?"

Lord Pembrooke's fear seemed to bleed away into anger. "If you are implying what I think you are implying, father..."

"I most certainly am!" His father answered, his

voice nearly a growl. "What else do you think could have happened to those jewels at this point?"

"They are missing, father, not stolen!"

"All of the evidence is against your theory, my boy," Lord Crettingham snarled, pointing at his son. "We searched this house high and low for the better part of the day, and what do we have to show for it?

He took a step toward his son, his eyes malicious. "You decided to have yourself a little glory the night that your friends came 'round, and one of them, realizing the immense worth that those diamonds hold, decided to nick them for themselves. And now, because of your choices, your bride and our family have been robbed of one of our greatest inheritances."

Lord Pembrooke could only stare at his father.

The others in the room felt horribly exposed, and could only glance between one another. Henrietta caught her brother's eye, and he could only shake his head. From frustration or disappointment, she could not be sure.

"You should be ashamed of yourself," Lord Crettingham added, his voice quieter, and yet much more authoritative. It came out almost like a hiss. "I truly believed you to be much wiser than you have proven yourself to be this evening."

Lord Pembrooke remained silent.

"See? You cannot even deny it, for you know that my words are the truth." When still no one spoke, Lord Crettingham scowled and with his hands balled into fists, made his way to the door.

    The next sound was a loud slam.

# Chapter 4
## THE PRAYER

Henrietta rose to her feet immediately and crossed the room to her beloved.

"Darling," she said softly, but he would not look at her. His eyes hovered over the door, as if he could not believe what had just occurred.

She grasped the sleeve of his jacket when he would not return her gaze. "You know as well as I do that not one of our friends would ever even consider taking something so precious to your family."

"She's right," Lady Charlotte added quietly. "I don't think any of them are capable of such jealous acts!"

They all nodded at one another.

Still, Lord Pembrooke remained silent. Henrietta felt her heart flutter in her chest, wondering how in the world she could help him.

"Brother, money is of little consequence to our little group," Lord William said, standing to his feet. "Surely you must know this."

Lord Pembrooke turned then on his brother, his senses apparently returning to him. His brow was tight and furrowed, and he glared at him. "William, surely you remember the true value of those jewels?"

Lord William appeared affronted. "How could I not? Father boasts of them any chance he can."

Lord Pembrooke sighed heavily, his shoulders tense. "It isn't the wealth that concerns me. Father is right. Those jewels represent connections to the royal family; they signify power."

"Are you inferring someone would wish them for what…a collector's piece?" Lord Boyle asked. "Something to show off to their friends at parties?"

Lord Pembrooke seemed to recoil at his words, and Lord Boyle noticed at once.

"I meant no harm –"

"And that still does not prove that one of our friends, our friends, my love, has taken them. Can you truly look at those around you and accuse them of theft?"

Lord Pembrooke looked down at his beloved, into her searching and hopeful eyes, and seemed to relax ever so slightly. He scanned the faces around him, from his frustrated brother who had his arms folded across his chest, to the ladies sitting together on the settee, to Henrietta's brother, who also seemed frustrated, standing beside the armchair.

"You're right," he said eventually, after a few moments of painful silence. "You are right, I'm sorry." He looked between the faces, who all seemed to relax as well. "I hope you can all forgive me for even allowing myself to entertain such terrible thoughts. "

"Of course we do," Lady Mary said. "It is only natural to be afraid when something so dear is missing."

"If you ask me, our family would likely be far better off if we had no such treasure in our possession," Lord William said. "Then we would never have found ourselves in this situation."

Lord Pembrooke sighed. "William, I do not believe that is the right attitude either."

"There can be nothing more done this evening," Lord Boyle said. "I think it would be wise for us to get our rest, for church will come early tomorrow, and everyone needs to be fresh and amiable."

"You're right," Lord Pembrooke said. "Let us get some rest."

The next morning came quickly, and Henrietta awoke with a heavy heart. She worried about where the jewels were, of course, but her primary concern was for her betrothed. As she sat on the edge of her bed, watching the sun start to streak through the trees outside the window, she realized that there had never been a time in her life when she had seen such fear on Lord

Pembrooke's face. She had never seen him so ashen, so pale, and so without words before.

She heard Lady Mary roll over in the bed beside hers, and turned to look at her. She felt a twinge of jealousy at the ease with which she and Lady Charlotte slept. They both looked so peaceful. How she longed to feel that way, especially so close to her wedding.

She slid down off the bed and positioned herself on her knees. She gazed out the window at the breathtaking scene that was unfolding before her, and felt a sense of peace wash over her.

She folded her hands, bent her head and closed her eyes.

*Lord*, she prayed, *there has been a great disturbance in this house in the last few days. We aren't sure what has happened, but it has caused great distress in my husband to be. I come humbly before You asking for Your help once more.*

*Please first and foremost, give us peace as we approach our wedding day. Help us to keep our sights on what truly matters.*

*And please give Daniel and his father the resolution they need. And lastly, if it be in Your will, please help us to find the jewels. Not because we want the wealth, but because I would like to put this all behind ourselves as a great misunderstanding.*

*Thank you for everything that you have done for us, for getting us this far, and for all that you will do for us in the days to come. In Jesus' name I pray, Amen.*

She sat in silence for a few moments, allowing the peace of her moment in prayer to envelope her.

She heard stirring, and when she looked over her shoulder, she saw Lady Charlotte stretching as she laid in her bed.

"Good morning," Henrietta whispered, smiling.

Lady Charlotte lifted her head and looked toward the window. "Oh, Henrietta. Good morning." She sat up. "Did you sleep quite all right?"

Henrietta nodded. "I did. And you?"

Lady Charlotte nodded, stifling a yawn. She noticed that Lady Mary still slept, so she quietly made her way to sit beside Henrietta on the floor.

Together they watched the sun flickering between the branches in the trees, sharing the moment together.

"Do you believe that someone could have taken the jewels?" Lady Charlotte asked quietly.

Henrietta glanced at her. "I do not. Do you?"

Lady Charlotte hesitated before she answered. "I...am not sure. I would very much like to believe that everyone is innocent."

"I cannot doubt my friends," Henrietta replied. "I cannot afford to become suspicious of those trying to help me prepare for marriage."

Lady Charlotte nodded. "I understand. Allow me, then, to worry about it for you."

Henrietta felt a familiar flicker of anxiety in her chest, and she took a deep breath to steady herself. "I don't want you to worry about it either."

Lady Mary began to roll in her bed once more.

Henrietta laid her hand over her friend's. "Come, let us rise and ready ourselves for church this morning."

Within the hour, two carriages were making their way down the quiet road towards the church, everyone bundled up in warmer clothing as the sun was not a great source of warmth that morning.

Everyone seemed in much better spirits than the night before, and by the time they reached the church, thoughts of the diamonds had almost left their minds entirely.

All except for Henrietta, who had been mulling over what Lady Charlotte had said that morning. Her deepest fear still was that one of their friends, people that they trusted above all others, had possibly stolen the jewels from them. The idea that it was even remotely possible, that she even questioned it, made her stomach turn over inside of herself.

The minister at the parish greeted her and Lord Pembrooke most warmly that morning, saying how delighted he was to be performing the ceremony for them in just a few days' time. He welcomed them to the front to share with the entire congregation who they were and the fact they were to be married. There was much rejoicing, especially from each of their friends. Henrietta smiled as she looked into each of their faces.

Who could it have been? Who could be smiling so widely and so happily up at them right now, knowing that their little secret was never to be discovered?

She paid little attention to the hymns they sang, and was nearly lost in her own thoughts as the minister began his sermon before the words he spoke caught her ear.

"…and in Exodus, we can see most clearly how the Lord despises a great number of atrocities of the heart. Murder, adultery, theft…"

She stared at him, wondering if perhaps the Holy Spirit inside her stirred, or if it was her own heart responding to his words. Theft? How strange he would choose to mention that, when there was such a question hanging over their own heads about it.

"I was troubled to hear that the Jefferson farm was once more a victim of theft; someone has been after their goats for a few months now, and their number has decreased drastically. I have felt it laid upon my spirit to discuss the importance of not only resisting temptation, but also to make things right if you have wronged someone else."

Henrietta could not believe her ears. How strange was it that the minister said words that she herself wished she could say to the person who perhaps had stolen her beloved's jewelry? Had someone told him? Was he aware of the fact that she felt that he was speaking directly to her?

He opened his Bible and continued speaking. "The Word has quite a lot to say about stealing. A few examples were as follows; 'Ye shall not steal, neither deal falsely, neither lie one to another,' in Leviticus chapter nineteen, verse eleven. And in Proverbs, chapter ten, verse two, 'Treasures of wickedness profit nothing.' And on several occasions, the Lord plainly says, 'Thou shalt not steal.' My dear friends, take heed the word of the Lord. Listen to it clearly. Stealing does not simply apply to criminals. We are all capable of it. Jealousy is a snare that all of us shall encounter in our lives, and we must be prepared to resist."

He looked around the room at those gathered, and continued. "If this is something that you have struggled with, or know of someone who has struggled with it, take heart. The Lord is faithful and just to forgive us. If we have wronged the Lord, first we must make it right with Him, accept his forgiveness, forgive ourselves, and then ask for forgiveness from those whom we have wronged. But what I wish to discuss this morning is how we can resist such a temptation, and how to prepare your hearts against the twisted claw of jealousy."

Henrietta realized she had been holding her breath. She attempted to appear as if she still listened to the minister, but her mind was far from him. Stealing does not simply apply to criminals. We are all capable of it.

Everyone who had been at the dinner party that Saturday evening was with them at church that morning, so they all had heard the very same thing that she had. Would they have listened in the same way that she had? Would it have struck a chord with them, causing them to immediately realize that they had done wrong?

She hoped against all hope, that if the very worst had happened, if one of their friends had betrayed them and stolen the jewels from right underneath her fiancé's nose, the person who had taken them would be so moved by the minister's sermon that morning, and return the jewels to their rightful place that afternoon.

At that point, she didn't even care who had done it; she couldn't bring herself to accuse anyone, not even in the deepest recesses of her mind. No one stuck out; no one seemed suspicious. All she hoped was that they would make it right, and they could be forgiven, and they could move forward with the wedding without any more trouble.

When they arrived home from church that afternoon, Henrietta watched each guest very closely. They enjoyed a wonderful afternoon together, with tea on the cobblestone terrace, dinner in the grand dining hall, and music and games in the evening together. If anyone ever left the group, they left in groups of two or more, never alone. She forced herself to be patient, to wait until just before heading to bed before she checked the cabinet one more time.

She told Lady Charlotte and Lady Mary that she was going to the washroom to freshen up before bed, and made a short detour to the sitting room.

The room was dark, all of the candles extinguished. She was thankful for a bright moon, for the room was easily navigated. She made her way to the cabinet, her heart slamming painfully against her ribcage. Pulling the doors open, she looked inside. It was dark, even with the light of the moon. She laid her hand inside, sweeping all along the shelves.

They were still gone.

She closed the door to the cabinet, leaning her back against it, sighing heavily.

She wasn't sure why she had believed in such a strong way that the thief would return the jewels. She had hoped that the message that morning had somehow stirred something deep inside them just like it had her, and that they would have been changed.

How fickle people were, she realized. She felt sorrow overtake her, and some tears spill from her eyes. She didn't know why she was allowing doubt to take control of her, doubt of her friends and their decisions. What could they gain, she wondered? What would the point be?

She made her way upstairs to her room, attempting to convince herself that she was being foolish, that of course none of her friends would have stolen the jewels. She was tired of the back and forth inside her mind, the fighting with herself. It was wearing on her, and she prayed once more for a resolution to the situation.

She heard footsteps down an adjacent hall from her room as she reached her door, and she noticed a dark shape in the distance. The moonlight allowed her to just make out his features.

"Lord William?" She whispered through the dark.

The shadow recoiled, and abruptly turned to face her.

"Lady Henrietta! My heavens you…startled me."

He took a few steps toward her. "What are you still doing up?"

"I...was just visiting the washroom. I suppose I was looking for a moment alone. There have been so many people around, you know," she said. The minister's words filled her mind once more. Ye shall not steal, neither deal falsely, neither lie one to another.

Conviction spread through her like fire. She had just done what she hoped other weren't doing to her and Lord Pembrooke.

He nodded. "Well, you are entitled to a moment of privacy in this busy time."

"What are you still doing awake? I thought you were the first to retire this evening."

Lord William nodded his head. "Yes, I was. I was simply parched, however, and needed to step out for a quick drink."

"Well, I won't keep you then," she replied, her hand on her doorknob. "Good night, Lord William."

"Of course," he said, bowing to her. "Have a good night, Lady Henrietta."

She let herself into her room, and both Lady Charlotte and Lady Mary were still awake.

"Who was that?" Lady Charlotte asked.

"Oh, just Lord William," Henrietta replied, collapsing onto the bed beside her friend.

"What was he doing out at this time?" Lady Mary asked, her brow furrowing.

"Getting something to drink, I think," Henrietta replied. "He asked me the very same thing."

Lady Mary stood to her feet, stretching her arms over her head. "We should get some sleep, my friends. I cannot believe how late it is already."

"Yes, I agree," Henrietta replied, also making her way to her side of the bed.

"It is strange that he asked why you were out of bed," Lady Charlotte said, looking at Henrietta. "Was he suspicious of you in some way?"

"I'm sure it was an innocent request," Lady Mary replied before Henrietta could. "Unless you are implying that he thinks Lady Henrietta took the jewels." At that, Lady Mary laughed out loud, covering her mouth with her hand.

Henrietta smiled in reply. "I certainly hope he doesn't suspect me! Why would I steal the jewels that I am to wear to my own wedding?"

Lady Charlotte shook her head. "That would be awfully preposterous."

They settled down soon after, and Henrietta listened to the sound of their quiet, even breathing as they both fell asleep.

She reflected on her encounter with Lord William in the hall. Did he perhaps think that she had taken the jewels herself? Had he been suspicious? Perhaps, if she were honest with herself, she would admit that she, too, was suspicious of him.

Could she trust no one? Was everyone just as likely as the rest? Did any of them actually suspect that she had been the one to take the diamonds?

Frustrated and wishing for answers, Henrietta fell into a fitful sleep, full of glittering jewels just out of reach, and cackling laughter just out of sight.

## Chapter 5
## THE LETTER

"I cannot take this any longer," Henrietta exclaimed as she stood to her feet.

It was two days before the wedding, and Henrietta and her friends were attempting to enjoy some peace and quiet outside on the lawn. Lord Pembrooke had gone into town with his father to the parish to speak with the minister about final wedding preparations. Never in her wildest dreams had she thought that preparing for a wedding would be as tedious as it was, and much of the joy had been stolen from her when she thought of the thief and the diamonds. She told herself time and time again that the diamonds didn't matter, that she didn't need them to be married, but no matter what she did, she could not escape the fear that plagued her because of their absence.

Perhaps she was haunted by Lord Pembrooke's

face, seeing the fear reflected in his eyes. Or perhaps it was the anger in Lord Crettingham's voice that still rung in her mind. Or perhaps even still it was the way that Lord William had openly wondered what she was doing out of bed so late last night.

She felt as if everything was falling apart around her, and that no one cared enough to admit it.

"What on earth is the matter?" Lady Charlotte asked, staring up at Henrietta. "What do you mean?"

Henrietta clenched her fists. "This…not knowing! I cannot stand it a moment longer."

Lady Mary rose to her feet and came to stood beside her friend, her arm around her shoulder. "Not knowing what? Come now, do try to calm yourself."

Henrietta sighed heavily. "The diamonds…I cannot help but still wonder what happened to them."

"Whatever for?" Lady Charlotte asked. "Lord Pembrooke said that we would continue the search for them after the wedding. Didn't you see the necklace that his mother procured for you to wear instead? I almost think that it is even prettier than the first one."

Henrietta slumped back into the chair she had vacated. "That's not it…" she replied. "I just can't believe that someone has taken them. I mean, who could do such a thing? Do they not know how it torments me, the idea of one of my friends betraying me so? Of betraying Lord Pembrooke? It is just…unthinkable!"

"I agree with you," Lady Charlotte said, coming

to kneel beside her chair. "It is unthinkable."

"But what if you worry for no reason?" Lady Mary added, looking down at the other two. "What if they simply are missing, and we just have not yet discovered them?"

Henrietta considered her words, and her heart lightened ever so slightly. "Do you really think so?" she asked, peering up into her friend's face. How much she hoped that she was right.

"Perhaps we haven't expended all of our options yet," Lady Charlotte said. "Are there any places we have not yet looked?"

"Not that I can think of," Henrietta replied, looking down at her hands clenched together tightly in her lap. "We practically tore the entire first floor apart looking for them. Remember?"

Lady Charlotte and Lady Mary both nodded their heads, glancing at each other.

"But is it possible in the rest of the manor that we have not considered?" Lady Charlotte added. "Perhaps Lady Mary is on the right track here."

"Where else could they be?" Henrietta asked.

"That's what we are asking you," Lady Mary replied.

"I don't know, I suppose we haven't looked upstairs. I mean, all of the bedrooms have been checked, and we checked our room, didn't we?"

"We did," Lady Mary said. "Looked under absolutely everything."

"See? Then we have no places left."

Lady Charlotte pursed her lips together. "Dear, I just had a thought. And I do not wish to trouble you with it, so please do hear me out before replying, all right?"

Henrietta, feeling a flush of concern, nodded her head.

"All right. What if…in all the excitement of everything going on, in the frustration and confusion, what if Lord Pembrooke misplaced them himself?"

Henrietta's first reaction was to be affronted. How could she say such a thing about her betrothed? But as she considered her words, she wondered if there was perhaps some truth to them.

"Then what are you proposing, exactly?" Henrietta replied.

Lady Charlotte smiled over her head at Lady Mary, who nodded encouragingly. Apparently, they had not anticipated for her to take it as well as she had.

"I…am not sure," Lady Charlotte replied. "Can you think of a place where he could have put it, a place where we wouldn't have even thought to look again?"

Henrietta looked between the girls. "Well, he told me that he looked everywhere he had thought of."

"What about in his study?" Lady Mary asked.

"I searched there myself," Henrietta replied.

"The library?" Lady Charlotte suggested.

"No, we spent the better part of two hours in there with Lord Boyle and Lord William," Lady Mary replied.

Henrietta pondered, mentally walking the long halls of Pembrooke Place.

"What about…his room?" she finally said, quietly.

"What?" Lady Charlotte asked, leaning closer.

"His room," she said again. "Could he have left them in his room?" She chewed on her bottom lip. "But he said that he never moved them after we looked at them that Saturday."

"Dear, even his father said that he has been so preoccupied with preparations for the wedding that he has forgotten many things."

Henrietta nodded her head. "It's true…He nearly forgot that he had to go into town today. He only remembered when I told him before breakfast."

"It wouldn't hurt for us to check," Lady Charlotte said.

"I don't know," Henrietta replied, suddenly feeling vulnerable. "I wouldn't feel right just going into his room to look around."

"Oh, my dear, he won't mind in the least if we somehow stumble upon the jewels in his room! Surely he would allow us if he were here for us to ask him," Lady Mary said.

"But he isn't here to tell us if it is okay for us to go into his room. That feels like a great invasion of privacy." Henrietta looked pleadingly up at the girls. Suddenly the idea of finding the jewels didn't seem as important.

"I agree with Lady Mary," Lady Charlotte said. "I do not believe he would mind."

Henrietta tugged at the lace seam on the front of her dress, indecisive. "You truly do not think he would mind?"

"Not if we find the diamonds, certainly not," Lady Charlotte said.

"All right. But let us hurry. I do not wish to be caught snooping around his private quarters."

"In two days, my dear, those will be your quarters as well," Lady Mary said.

Her fears assuaged, the three ladies returned to the manor, leaving the pleasant air and afternoon behind.

The house itself was silent, all of the staff and remaining guests preoccupied in other apparent matters, for which Henrietta was immensely grateful. She knew that she had no reason to feel as if she was sneaking around, for this house was to be hers the day after tomorrow, but somehow the pressure of what they were about to do weighed heavily on her heart.

A door closed not far down the opposite hall where they walked, and Henrietta jumped, clutching her gloved hand over her now thundering heart.

"Easy, dear, are you All right?" Lady Charlotte asked, her voice quiet.

Henrietta nodded. She wanted to finish this endeavor as soon as they possibly could.

The door to Lord Pembrooke's room loomed at the end of the hall, directly across from Lord William's. A large window was set into the far wall between the doors, the warm sunlight filtering in, and it eased Henrietta's nerves ever so slightly.

They reached the door, and both Lady Charlotte and Lady Mary looked at Henrietta.

"What?" She asked.

Lady Charlotte gestured at the door. "It is your room, after all, you should be the one to go in."

She swallowed painfully. "Well, it's not mine yet."

"It's as good as," Lady Mary whispered. "Come on, let's not waste any time."

She grasped the door handle, steadied herself with a deep breath, and pushed the door open.

The room itself was darker than the hall, with the velvet blinds drawn over the windows. She hesitantly took a step inside, and was pleased to find that the scent in the room was rather pleasant, like pine trees and cinnamon. She knew that he loved cinnamon tea, and the thought drew a smile to her face.

Then the guilt returned. What would he say if he knew that she had snuck inside his room without permission?

"Come now, let us search," Lady Mary said, pushing her way into the room from behind Henrietta. She crossed quickly to the windows and threw the drapes open, flooding the room with warm, orange light. It brought the whole place to life, with a lush four poster bed now easily visible, adorned with a hand-stitched quilt and a velvet canopy. There was a rich cherry wood wardrobe in the far corner, the mirror on the front reflecting some of the sunlight back into the room. And there was a large portrait across from the door beside one of the windows; a winding dirt road, dense forests, and single carriage on its way at what looked to be a leisurely pace.

She took a few steps toward it, wondering what he saw in the painting. Was it the ease it brought? Was it the motion? Was it the colors? Henrietta felt there was much more about Lord Pembrooke that she needed to learn.

"Where do you expect they could be?" Lady Charlotte asked, standing uncomfortably holding her arms close to herself on the opposite side of the room.

"Drawers, out of sight," Henrietta said, and it was almost as if she heard someone else murmur the words.

The other women remained silent until she looked up at them.

"Oh, I'm sorry," she shook her head to clear it. "I imagine they would be quite obvious unless they were put away somewhere."

"You are probably right," Lady Charlotte said. "I'll start over here in the desk by the door."

"And I'll start with this little table here," Lady Mary said, gesturing to a small, round table with a small drawer tucked in the corner. She gazed around the room. "Why don't you search his bedside table?" She suggested, pointing to the little set of drawers nestled beside the bed.

"Good thinking," Lady Charlotte said, agreeing.

Henrietta made her way over to the drawers, knelt down beside them, and began to pull the drawers open.

The top drawer contained nothing special; a knife, some extra candles for the chamberstick on top of the table. She also found a slender book. She grinned when she realized that it was one that she had read many times.

Both of the other ladies made passing comments about their lack of findings, and they all continued their search.

The second drawer held a letter opener and a few handkerchiefs. Growing more anxious by the moment, she pulled open the bottom drawer and was surprised when she saw it completely full of letters, all opened, tucked neatly inside.

She immediately recognized her own handwriting, and smiled as she realized that he must have kept all of her letters. She gently touched them with her fingertips, a rush of affection filling her heart for, Daniel. How tender and sweet he was, how romantic. And he did not know that she knew.

Beside her letters, she noticed a different set of letters, and those appeared to be in his hand. More intrigued than anything, she lifted one from the drawer.

My dearest love, the letter began.

How strange, she thought to herself. That was not the name that he used for her. Perhaps that is why the letter was never sent? Perhaps he thought it too brash or forward? She bent her nose back over the letter and continued to read.

I have longed to see you. The nights have been long and the days like a lifetime. I only wish that all of the appointments that I have no longer existed so I could spend my time with you alone.

*That sounded much more like him*, she thought.

I hope you can forgive me for the fact that it has been so long since my last letter. There has been much activity going on with the wedding approaching, and I have had little time to sneak away and be alone.

She felt a prick of fear like ice in her heart. Why would he say that it has been long since his last letter? He wrote to her at least twice a week, and why did he mention the wedding in such an offhanded manner?

"What's the matter?" Lady Charlotte asked.

Henrietta did not look up, but she assumed that

her concern was clear on her face. But she had to keep reading.

To answer your question, yes, I believe that everything is still unknown. She suspects nothing, and of course we both know the marriage is for convenience only. The playful banter between us is no different than a bard's tale in a tavern. You know that my heart only beats for you.

The wedding is just in a few short days, and once it is over, I will send a letter to you at once. We can then arrange a meeting of some sort, and I will simply tell my wife that I have business in town. Then we can finally enjoy each other's company once more.

Remember that you always have my heart, and always will.

Always, Daniel

She glanced at the date of the letter, her heart colliding with her rib cage like a bird in captivity. It had only been written three days prior, and he had used his given name!

"W...what?" she breathed, holding the letter away from herself as if it was something rotting and putrid.

"What is it?" Lady Charlotte asked, coming to her side. She knelt down beside her, and with no resistance, was able to take the letter from Henrietta's hand.

She quickly scanned the letter as Lady Mary joined them.

Henrietta felt as if she were about to go out of her mind with anguish. Her Lord Pembrooke? In love with another woman?

"Has he...taken another lover?" Lady Mary asked, reading the letter over Lady Charlotte's shoulder.

"It appears that way..." Lady Charlotte replied quietly, as if saying it too loudly might disturb Henrietta.

"I...he..." Henrietta said, the words unable to form properly, taking the letter once more from Lady Charlotte. "What does this mean?" she whispered, pointing to the scrawling script across the parchment.

The other two women looked at each other, and then back up at their friend. The fact that neither of them could produce any sort of encouragement or wisdom is what made her realize that this was not just a dream.

The tears burst from her eyes as if they had waited there all along, and she hopped to her feet. Anger and sorrow fought for control of her heart, and the pain was just too much to bear. The letter still clutched tightly in her hands, she ran from the room as fast as she could carry herself.

She didn't stop, and she hated the fact that she knew exactly how to escape from the manor. It took no effort to find her way back down the hall from whence they came, and it wasn't until she collided with something very solid did she look up.

The face of Lord William gazed down into her tear streaked face. His eyes were wide with concern, and immediately his hands were on her shoulders, steadying her.

"Dear heavens, girl, whatever is the matter with you? You look as pale as parchment."

He must have noticed the parchment in her hands, for she did not speak.

"What is that?" he asked, gesturing to it.

She shook her head, more tears fluttering down her cheeks.

"Come now, I cannot help you if you do not tell me." He peered at her very gently, his eyes cautious. "Take a deep breath to steady yourself, there you are."

Henrietta managed to take a shaky breath, and the shuttering sobs subsided momentarily.

"There, now. Tell me what happened. Are the wedding nerves finally catching up with you?"

Anger flushed her cheeks and she clenched her fists once more, the parchment crinkling in her palm.

"No…your brother…he…" she began, and unable to say the words out loud, shoved the letter into Lord William's hands.

It only took him a moment to finish reading, and when he looked at her, his eyes were wide with disbelief.

"Lady Henrietta, you mustn't believe this," he started, but she shook her head violently.

"Then what do you propose I believe, Lord

William? Surely this letter was not intended for me. He apparently meant to send this any day now, and never meant for anyone to see it."

Lord William's eyes narrowed, his head tilting to the side. "Where did you find this letter?"

Henrietta shook her head once more. "That matters not. What does matter is that your brother does not love me. He loves another woman, and I am not about to marry a man who will begin our marriage in the most unfaithful way that a man could."

She snatched the letter from his grip, glared at him for even being related to Lord Pembrooke, and straightened herself up.

Down the hall, she could hear Lady Charlotte and Lady Mary calling for her.

Her strength and courage returning, the anger currently winning control, she shoved past Lord William and down the hall.

"Where are you going?" Lord William called after her. "You can't leave! The wedding is in two days!"

"The wedding is off!" She cried in return, the tears welling up in her eyes once more, feeling as if they might spill out at any moment. But she wouldn't allow them to. Lord Pembrooke didn't deserve her tears. Not after what he had done to her.

## Chapter 6
## STARLIGHT AND SECRETS

She reached home before long, and was not particularly surprised to know that Lady Mary and Lady Charlotte had followed her.

Her parents were the most surprised to see her home, and she spent the better part of the afternoon sobbing into her father's shoulder, the letter a wrinkled, tattered mess after everyone else had the pleasure of reading it.

By evening, the house had settled into an uneasy silence, the disbelief on everyone's lips, but Henrietta would not listen to any of them. She didn't dare give her heart any sort of hope about the situation.

She loved Lord Pembrooke above any man she had ever met, and never in her wildest dreams had she ever suspected he could have so blatantly discarded her feelings like that. She locked herself away in her room, and despite the urgent pounding on the door from her friends and her mother, she would not come out.

The letter that had so changed her life stayed within arm's reach, and she stared at it for so long that her eyes grew sore. How was it that in her efforts to set things right before her wedding, she inadvertently sabotaged herself? The worry for the jewels seemed as if it had happened years before, and she wondered why she ever cared so much about them in the first place. It was interesting to her how the mind could make such a big deal out of something so insignificant when something so horrible was happening just under her nose?

She wondered if she knew the woman. She thought back to any and all of the balls that she and Lord Pembrooke had ever attended together, naming each and every acquaintance she could remember to herself. None of them seemed particularly charming, but that didn't mean that she and Lord Pembrooke were not well versed in hiding their feelings in front of others. For certain, he had successfully hidden this relationship from her for as long as he had, however long that actually was, and she would have remained unaware of it if she had not stumbled upon the letter in his room.

In all fairness, she never should have found the letter. But if she had not, she would have married a man who cared little for her or her heart, and immediately would be breaking his marriage vows. Did his faith and his integrity really mean so little to him? How could he look at her and say such sweet things and not mean them?

Faith.

Before another dark thought passed through her mind, she knelt to her knees in front of her window. The moon had just begun to ascend into the sky, the bright, milky light surrounded by pinpricks of stars. If her heart was not so distressed, she would have been able to fully appreciate the beauty.

*Lord*, she prayed in the deepest recesses of her heart, her head cradled in her hands. *There are no words for what I feel right now. I am so grateful that You already know all, for I do not wish to utter one more word about what has happened today. My heart feels as if it has been beaten, ripped apart, and tossed out into the frigid night. I do not understand what Your plan is, nor do I understand what happened today. I just know that I cannot handle it a moment longer.*

*All I ask for is Your peace and Your grace. You are my fortress, my deliverer, and my Savior. There is nothing I can do apart from You. And in order to get through the foreseeable future in my life, in order to pick up all of the pieces that have been shattered beyond recognition, I need You to carry me.*

There was a sharp rap of knuckles on her door, and she glared at the wooden surface.

"Go away," she cried. "I already told you to leave me be."

"Henrietta?"

Her hands fell to her lap, and she nearly fell over. She felt as if her heart stopped all together.

Lord Pembrooke?

She stared at the door, breathing very quickly, and

she looked all around. Did she...did she just imagine his voice in her anguish?

"Henrietta, please, can I come inside?"

She rose to her feet immediately and crossed the distance to her door. She nearly pulled the door open for him, but a twinge of fear caused her to hesitate.

"What are you doing here?" she said, and it came out rather quietly. Her eyes stung, and after she had thought she had cried all of the tears she possibly could, she was surprised to feel more of them fill her eyes.

"I need to come in. We need to talk," he replied calmly.

She could almost imagine his face. His brows furrowed, his lips taut, his jaw clenched.

"No," she replied before the thoughts had formed in her mind. "There is nothing you can say. I found the letter."

"What letter?" he asked, exasperated. The tone that he took made her realize that he must have said those words many more times today than just in that moment.

She debated with herself for several moments before she recognized the fact that this conversation would need to happen at some point, and it might as well happen now while all of her arguments were fresh in her mind.

She pulled the door open and fastened her best

glare on her face as she looked into his face, but it was immensely difficult. In the low light from the candles lit around her room, the anxiety was evident upon his face. She had not prepared herself for seeing him, and it nearly made her lose her nerve.

She turned and walked across her room to the chair beside her window where she had just been, seated herself upon it, and gazed out the window.

Lord Pembrooke hesitated by the door, and took a few steps inside. When she didn't look up at him, which took all of her strength, he cleared his throat.

"What in the world has happened?" he asked quietly, his voice barely a whisper.

She did not answer him.

"I come home from town after having a lovely talk with the minister about the wedding to find that my fiancée has left in a horrendous rage, going on about a letter that she discovered, and that our wedding has been called off?"

She could feel his gaze on the side of her face, but she focused her gaze on the moon outside.

"You must speak to me, Henrietta, for I have no earthly idea what is going on at all."

She whipped around and glared at him, her eyes narrow. "Do not use my Christian name, you have no right to it any longer."

"What do you mean?" He asked quickly, the color

in his cheeks deepening. "My brother told me everything that happened, and I still do not understand –"

"Do not come here and pretend to be the innocent one!" Henrietta replied, standing to her feet now, her hands clenched tightly at her side, her voice rising. "I found this," she said, holding up the tear stained letter, "in your room this afternoon. You can stop the farce; I discovered your secret."

"What secret?" He asked, the astonishment clear on his face. "That I have a lover? How can you believe something so preposterous? And what, may I ask, were you doing in my room?"

"It would have been my room as well in two days' time," she retorted angrily, repeating Lady Mary's words to him. "And I was looking for these jewels that disappeared, thank you very much. But stop trying to avoid the subject! You have taken a lover, and I would have been completely unaware of it had I not discovered this letter!"

"You keep saying these things, and I will continue to tell you that you are wrong! I have no one in my life aside from you! What need would I have for another woman?"

She shook her head angrily. "I do not know, why don't you enlighten me?" she replied.

She noticed his hands clench and loosen. He was growing angry as well. *Good,* she thought. *Maybe he will finally tell me the truth.*

"So after all of this time, after knowing me for

our entire lives, you just now decide that I am a liar and am capable of such deceit?"

These words caused her pause, and she rubbed the letter between her fingers. "Isn't that what people do when they are trying to cover up something? They act and pretend as if everything is normal?"

"I cannot believe this…" he said, pressing the bridge of his nose with his forefinger and thumb. "After all we have been through, it is baffling me how little you really think of me." He looked squarely at her. "I do not have a lover, not apart from you. You are the only woman I have ever loved and the only woman I have ever wanted to love."

Oh, how she wanted to believe him. How she wanted to just throw herself into his arms and be done with the whole thing, to put it all behind them.

When she didn't reply, he held out his hand.

"Now, give me the letter."

She took a step back, clutching the letter close to herself. "No, I don't want to."

"Why not? I want to see exactly what it is that I have been accused of."

She watched his face. Would his face betray something that his words would not as he read the letter through? He waited patiently as she decided.

She passed him the letter and watched as he unfolded it. He held it as if it was something disgusting.

She watched him carefully as his eyes scanned the letter, yet his eyes remained curious and his brow furrowed. Perhaps he was a much better actor than she had ever realized.

He lowered the letter and sighed.

She braced herself. Here it comes, the truth, she told herself.

"This is not my letter," he replied flatly, looking down at the letter once more.

"Then how can you explain that it was in your room?"

"Where did you find this?" Lord Pembrooke asked, shaking the letter gently.

Henrietta crossed her arms over her chest. "In the side table beside your bed."

The statement seemed perplexing to him. "Well, I keep my letters from you in there," he replied, and then rubbed his chins with his free hand, his eyes on the floor. "But I did not write this letter."

She rolled her eyes.

"It was lying right in the drawer beside my letters," Henrietta replied.

He looked back down at the letter, reading it through once more. Henrietta could only stand there and watch him, wondering what in the world was going through his mind. Was he about to admit that he had been discovered? There really was no way he could escape the truth now.

"This is not my handwriting," he said eventually, still studying the letter intently.

"I beg your pardon?" she asked, the humor lost to her.

He looked up at her, and pointed down to the letter. "This isn't my handwriting," he repeated.

"It is indeed your handwriting," she said slowly, peering carefully at him. Had he lost his mind? "I have received more than enough letters to recognize your handwriting."

"Yes, but I more than aware of how I write, and have been for my entire life, and this is not my handwriting."

"You must be joking," she replied. "It is your handwriting! It is!"

"I must admit that it is quite the striking resemblance, and I can certainly see how you could easily mistake it for mine," he said, looking up at her. "But I assure you. This letter was not written by me."

"There is no possible way that you can explain that."

"Find me one of my letters," he replied.

"What?" she asked.

"Find me one of the letters that I wrote to you." He paused. "You still have them, don't you? Or have you already thrown all of those into the fire?"

The pain in his voice stung her, and she shook her head.

"No, I didn't throw them into the fire. They're right over here."

She crossed the room to her desk underneath the opposite window and pulled the most recent letter that he had sent her from a tall stack of papers. She returned to Lord Pembrooke with it, and handed it to him.

He opened the letter, and a small smile pulled at the corner of his mouth, but she realized that it was a sad smile. He continued to read for a moment before he nodded.

"Here," he said, pointing to the word time in the letter she had just handed him. "Do you see how I write my letter T? Here tail of the T swoops down ever so slightly underneath the word. As it does on every letter T in this letter."

He pulled the other letter out once more, and pointed to another letter T, this time on the word activity. "Do you see how they are different? Here the T does not drop down below the other letters. It's a subtle difference, but it is there."

Henrietta sighed. "Perhaps I misunderstand you. You wish for me to believe that this other letter was not written by you because one of one tiny little difference?"

He shook his head. "Please go get me another letter, and I will prove that this is different."

She obeyed, and returned with a few more. Together they bent over the letters that he had spread out over the table beside her door, and he moved a few candles nearer so the letters could be seen more clearly.

Hope had begun to flicker in her chest. His calm had helped her to see that perhaps she was wrong, and that this letter was not actually written by him. The closer they looked and compared the one letter to all of the rest of his that he had sent, it seemed more and more that it was different.

She crossed her arms and stood a little ways back from the table. "How do I know that you aren't changing your handwriting ever so slightly so that you do not get caught?"

He rolled his eyes and sighed heavily, his palms rested on the table.

"Why in the world would I go to all of that trouble just to change a slight thing about it? Certainly if this was something I was doing, wouldn't I change it drastically so that no one could pin the letter on me or believe that I had written it if it ever was found?"

His logic seemed sound, and certainly he had a reason and answer for every question she had asked him, and they all made sense.

"That would just be a poor decision, and eventually lead to a predictable mistake, no matter what way you look at it."

There was little left in her mind to doubt him, and she felt an enormous relief wash over herself.

"Do you promise me that you didn't write this letter?" she asked quietly, pointing to it.

Lord Pembrooke looked at her, and then he turned his whole body to face her, taking her face in his hands. He tilted her chin up towards him so she could not look away.

"I swear on my very life that I did not write that letter."

There was nothing but honesty in his eyes, she realized, and she lost all of her strength. Her knees gave way, and she was thankful that he was already holding her, for she collapsed into his waiting arms.

The guilt and the grief of the day resurged and she cried into his shoulder as he held onto her.

How could she have been such a fool? How could she have really believed that he would have wronged her? Perhaps the idea was so great and so terrible that her fears had made something out of nothing and she allowed herself to be carried away by it.

"I'm sorry. I'm so sorry," she kept saying, unable to contain the rush of emotions washing over her. She felt so ashamed of herself and her ability to doubt him so easily.

"It's all right," he said, stroking her long hair which had come loose from its plait. "Don't worry, it's okay now…" he whispered.

They stood like that for a long time as they allowed the distance between themselves to lessen, the distance that she had created. She allowed him to love on her and whisper things in her ears to help her feel better.

*I do not deserve a love such as this*, she thought. *He has already forgiven me for ripping him to pieces. How must he have felt to be on the receiving end of my actions?*

The moon was no longer visible through the windows when she calmed down and they made proper amends.

"I'm sorry I ever thought that you could do that to me," she said, hoping that he knew just how much she meant with those words.

He smiled and nodded. "It is quite all right. I would have been just as frightened had the situation been one I had experienced in your place. I cannot blame you for reacting the way you did." He leaned closer to her. "In fact, it shows me the depth of your love for me, and how careful I should be in the future."

She smiled at his teasing and looked into his eyes.

"I'm sorry I went into your room without your permission," she added.

He hugged her more tightly and kissed the top of her head. "My dear, it is quite all right. You were right after all; it will be yours in just a matter of hours. Tomorrow we will be the Lord and Lady Pembrooke, and nothing could make me happier. There is nothing that I will ever wish to hide from you. Besides, I am glad that you thought to look in a place where I might have forgotten to check."

"It still was an invasion of your privacy," she replied into his sleeve.

He pulled away to look at her, smiling. "There is nothing that I wish to keep private from you, my love. I do ask, however, that you and I talk about things before you get so worried next time, all right?"

She nodded, and he brushed another tear from her cheek.

"Now," he said, untangling his arms from around her and walking back over to the table. "The question that remains is who wrote this letter?"

Henrietta pursed her lips. "I...don't know. I never gave it a thought that someone else could have written it. But then, why would it be in your room?" she wondered.

His brow furrowed once more, and she was appreciative that it was not because of her this time. "That is what concerns me, love. If someone else wrote it and put it in my room..." he sighed heavily. "It means that there are devious matters at play here."

"Whatever do you mean?" she asked.

"Someone went to great lengths to copy my handwriting, almost precisely. Someone created this letter with a purpose, and the only purpose that I can think of is to cause a rift between you and me."

She gasped. "But why? It very nearly worked!"

He shook his head. "I do not know, but I see no

alternate reason. Someone must have planted that letter in my room."

"How did they know you wouldn't just find the letter and be done with it?"

"They must have realized it would have bothered me so much that eventually I would have said something to you. And even if you didn't believe it, it would still cause a problem between us."

Henrietta sighed heavily. "This all seems very bizarre, especially since it happened right after the jewels went missing."

Lord Pembrooke's eyes grew wide. "Henrietta, you may be onto something there."

She looked at him, the same realization coming upon her. "You don't think…that the person who wrote the letter —"

"Must be the same person that stole the diamonds, of course!" he answered for her.

"What if the letter was planted as a distraction?" Henrietta asks. "We have been looking so hard for the jewels, perhaps the letters were to throw us off the scent?"

He scratched at his chin. "That would stand within reason," he replied. "Perhaps they believed we would forget about them if there was a disagreement between us."

"I could not have cared less about those

diamonds earlier today when I found the letter."

Lord Pembrooke smiled. "I think that perhaps the person who planted the letter did not suspect that you would have discovered the letter. It must have been intended for me to find, and then distract me well enough. Yes, that must be it."

Henrietta shook her head. "Do you believe the jewels are still in the manor?"

Lord Pembrooke looked as if he were going to answer, and then he exhaled. He smiled at her. "Let's forget about the jewels. The important thing is that you and I were far too clever for their little trick, and at this point, your love and my marriage to you is far more important than some rocks on a necklace."

She smiled up at him.

"If they wished to have taken the jewels that badly, then let them have them."

"What of your father?" Henrietta asked hesitantly.

Lord Pembrooke shook his head. "I wouldn't worry too much about it. He knows that our marriage is more important. He realized that he overreacted last week about them. He apologized already, and I believe he would agree with me about this, especially after he hears about this letter."

"Well, if you say so," Henrietta replied.

He kissed her on her forehead before retreating towards the door. "I must return home. I will see you at the altar, my love."

"So soon?" she said sadly.

He glanced out the window. "It is quite near midnight. We will be together again soon." He closed the door before peering inside once more.

"Thank you for not giving up hope," he said.

Her eyes filled with tears, and she laughed. "Of course my love. Thank you for not losing all hope in me."

"Never," he replied, and with another wide grin, he was gone.

## Chapter 7
## THE WEDDING

"Do you, Lady Henrietta Boyle, take –"

"No!"

The voice rang out in the full room like the strike of a bell. Henrietta and Lord Pembrooke stood at the front of the room before the minister. She held a bouquet of beautiful roses, and his coat had a single red rose pinned to the front. Her dress was a lovely pale blue, and his coat a deep, rich, burgundy. Never before had they thought the other looked more handsome.

All of the faces, including those of the bride and groom, turned to see Lord William standing to his feet from the second pew, livid color flooding his cheeks. His teeth were clenched, his eyes wild.

"What is the meaning of this?" the minister asked Lord William.

"I object!" Lord William said loudly, slamming his hands against the pew in front of himself in rage, causing those seated in front of him to nearly jump out of the pew.

"No, I object!" cried another voice. From behind Henrietta, the voice of Lady Mary rang out into the room.

Despair filled Henrietta as she turned to face her friend. "What?" she asked, looking at her.

Lady Mary was breathing heavy and her cheeks were bright red. She looked as if she might burst at any moment.

"I cannot believe you still decided to marry him," Lady Mary hissed through her teeth like a snake, her eyes narrow slits, her jaw set tight.

Henrietta could only stare at her.

"This is all your fault!" Lord William hollered, and Henrietta was surprised to see him pointing at Lady Mary.

"My fault?" she shrieked. "It wasn't my fault that Lord Pembrooke followed after Lady Henrietta the day before last!"

"But it wasn't my fault that he ended up seeing her that night, now was it?"

"Please, would someone remove these two from the room so we may resume the ceremony?" the minister asked.

A few men from each family rose in their seats and grabbed the two who continued to argue, their cries echoing in the vaulted ceiling.

Lord Pembrooke's grip tightened around Henrietta's hand.

"Wait," he said, just before the two were taken outside. He looked earnestly at Henrietta for a moment, ensuring she was aware of him, and he walked back down the aisle to where the men stood with his brother and Lady Mary.

Lord Pembrooke stared at his brother as if he were staring at a strange who was a criminal.

"What have you done, brother?" he said, his voice curt and quiet, but it carried across the room that was as silent as a tomb.

Lord William was breathing fast and heavy, looking wildly around the room, not meeting his brother's gaze, which was unshaking.

Eventually his gaze settled on Henrietta, and she saw a deep sadness written on the creases around his eyes. She saw a shining reflection, and realized that he wept.

"Lady Henrietta I…" he began, apparently ignoring the entire rest of the church. "I am absolutely and unashamedly in love with you."

There were gasps around the room, followed by fervent whispering.

He didn't seem to hear, and Lord Pembrooke looked just as startled as Henrietta felt.

"I have always loved you, ever since we were

children, even before my brother was to marry you. I didn't even understand what it all meant until we were older and I realized that no matter how much I wanted to marry you and to be your husband that I never would be able to. There would never be a place in the world where you and I could be together when my brother was in the picture."

Lord Pembrooke took a step towards his brother, bearing down on him, but Lord William continued before he could speak.

"I had hope once, however, that one summer in Brighton, do you remember it?"

To her surprise, she knew exactly what summer he spoke of. It was much warmer than usual, and her family and his took a trip when she was a young teenager. Lord Pembrooke had fallen quite ill that trip, and so she had spent a good portion of the time with his brother, whom she had enjoyed immensely.

"We had the most amazing time. I felt for sure that you must have felt the same way about me at the end of that week as I had felt about you for the entirety of my existence. When we returned home, however, you resumed your relationship with my brother. Yet I hoped, and have hoped all this time, that perhaps that one summer meant as much to as you as much as it did to me, and you simply were going to marry my brother out of duty, and that perhaps, deep down, your heart truly belonged to…me."

She could only stare at him. She had never, in the entire time she had known Lord William, ever suspected that his relationship with her was more than an amiable friendship. She had never even imagined there to be anything else. She had always enjoyed her time with him, but now...

Lord Pembrooke, the rage evident on his face now, grabbed his brother by the shoulders. "Get him out of my sight," he spat.

"Wait!" Lord William called over his shoulder, his eyes pleading with Henrietta. "Wait, please, I cannot let you go! Not like this! Please! Henrietta, choose me! Choose me, and we can live a long and happy life together!"

The shock of his statement caused Lord Pembrooke to cease his struggle against Lord William and simply stare at him.

There were many in the room who had turned to look up at Henrietta, who still stood at the altar, Lady Charlotte standing beside her, grasping her hand tightly, tears streaming down her gentle face. It was a comfort that one of her friends was still a true friend.

Lord Pembrooke even turned to look up at her, as if waiting for a response from her. Did he really believe that after all they had been through, after everything that had discussed the night before last, that she would ever back out on him for any reason?

"Lord William," she began, but even by the tone of her voice he knew, for he scowled and shook his head, looking down. "While I appreciate the sentiment, I apologize if any of my actions ever led you to believe that I felt anything romantic about our relationship. I love your brother, and I always have. I...I'm sorry," she ended.

Lord Pembrooke smiled tenderly at her, still restraining his brother, and Lord William's face was blotchy and streaked with tears.

Henrietta looked over at her friend. "And what of you, Lady Mary?"

Lady Mary looked between her and Lord Pembrooke and burst into tears, covering her face with her hands. Her wails echoed around the room, and then came her words.

"I have loved Lord Pembrooke since I met him," she sobbed. "He was always so kind to me, so generous. No other man has ever treated me the way that he did." She pulled her hands from her face and pointed angrily up at Henrietta. "You never treated him the way he should have been treated! You took him for granted! He worshipped the ground you walk on and you didn't even notice!"

She resumed her crying.

Henrietta felt as if she had been bludgeoned in the stomach with a boulder. How in the world could this have happened? Lady Mary was one of her very dearest friends. How could she have turned against her so vehemently?

"How did this happen?" Lord Pembrooke asked.

"We...we were at a ball one night, Lord William and I, and you two, of course," Lady Mary said between sobs, "And we stood outside, all alone, because the people we wanted to be dancing with were dancing with each other."

Lord Pembrooke handed his brother to the man who had grabbed him originally. "And?" he asked him, staring down into his face. "Tell me what happened so I can know that I am right in my suspicions."

Lord William had a hard time breaking eye contact with his brother, but he looked at his feet before continuing. "Lady Mary and I discovered that our desire was the same; in order for us to be with who we loved, you and Lady Henrietta had to be separated."

There were more murmurs from other guests in the room.

"So we came up with a plan. We decided to steal the diamonds that Lady Henrietta was to wear the day of the wedding."

Now Lord Crettingham, who had been staring speechless at his two sons, stood to his feet. "You stole the jewels?!" he cried. He crossed the room to his sons. "So not only are you a troublemaker, but you are a thief?" He straightened his shoulders and puffed out his chest. "You should be ashamed of yourself."

Lord William grimaced once more.

"What point was there in stealing the jewels?" Lord Pembrooke asked.

Lord William sneered. "I believed that you would never have married without the jewels," he began. "I believed if those disappeared that you would take it as a bad omen, or you would suspect each other of stealing the diamonds and it might tear you apart. And then I would step in and comfort Lady Henrietta from the angry Daniel. And to ensure I wasn't discovered, I made sure only to take them once you had showed them to all of your friends. I hoped that you would suspect them all before you ever suspected me."

"Well you were wrong, obviously, about me marrying without the jewels," Lord Pembrooke said. "And let me ask one more thing. Were you two the ones who planted that fake letter in my room?"

Lady Mary made a strangled whimpering sound.

Henrietta gasped. "You! You were the one who suggested we continue to search the house! And you gave me the idea of searching in Lord Pembrooke's room!"

Lady Mary hung her head, and Lady Charlotte huffed.

"If she had done her job better, then we wouldn't be in this mess!" Lord William spat, seething, in Lady Mary's direction.

Like a viper, her head shot up and she scowled at him. "If you would have copied his handwriting better, then –"

"Enough!" Lord Crettingham cried, and the room went silent. He turned on his younger son, who cowered in fear. "Where are the diamonds now?"

Lord William glanced over at Lady Mary.

Lord Crettingham seemed to take the hint, and rounded on her. "Where are they!"

Without another word, she held out her bag to him, hiding her face away. Lord Crettingham snatched it from her hands, pulled it open, and drew out the gleaming, sparkling diamonds.

There were gasps and cries of pleasure and awe.

Lord Crettingham also found the ring, and handed both of them to Lord Pembrooke, and bowed to him.

"These belong to you and to your bride, my son."

Lord Pembrooke nodded, and accepted them.

Lord William scowled at the two of them.

Lord Crettingham turned back to the two miscreants. "This is a holy event, a place where a marriage between two people who love each other and promise to do so for the rest of their lives is supposed to take place. You both will pay for what pain you have caused two innocent people. And trust me, I will ensure that justice is enacted."

Both Lord William and Lady Mary looked sadly at one another, their struggle at an end.

"Take them away. They do not deserve to be here," Lord Crettingham said scathingly. And without another word, they were removed from the room.

Lord Crettingham walked back down the aisle with Lord Pembrooke, who was now rather pale now that the excitement had died down. He still held the gleaming diamond jewels in his hands, and he returned to stand in front of Henrietta.

"Are you all right?" He asked her, searching her face.

"I..." she began. She shrugged her shoulders. "I do not know. That is a lot to take in."

He nodded in agreement, the understanding clear on his face. If she was so stricken to have been betrayed by such a good friend, he must feel just as anguished at having been betrayed by his own brother.

The minister looked between the two of them. "Do you wish to continue with the ceremony?"

"Just a moment," Lord Pembrooke said. He removed the necklace that Henrietta was wearing and handed it to Lady Charlotte. Then, he took the diamond necklace and put it around Henrietta's neck.

When he stepped back, many people in the room murmured to one another, and she realized how stunning it must look. He held up the diamond ring to her.

"Now, we are ready to continue," he said.

And she smiled up at him. For their marriage was more important than anything else that had happened. That much was clear now.

They finished the ceremony with much fanfare, with loud cheers and clapping from their remaining family and friends. Lady Charlotte hugged her fervently, with a mixture of joy and sadness on her face. They would have to discuss what had happened at some point, but they both knew it could wait.

They allowed everyone to congratulate them and wish them well, and they both felt at peace. What had happened was entirely out of their control, and they were not going to let the two who had attempted to sabotage their wedding to rob them of their joy on their wedding day.

Before the sun set that evening, Lord Pembrooke and his new wife were ushered into a carriage to head off on their honeymoon. Lord Pembrooke had planned an elaborate trek around the south of England, and they were to be gone celebrating for three weeks.

After waving at everyone excitedly, and their parents reassuring that they would handle everything at home, including Lady Mary and Lord William, they both leaned back in the carriage and sighed heavily.

"What a day," Henrietta said.

Lord Pembrooke smiled at her. "My dear bride, are you quite all right?"

"I am now," she replied honestly. "It is all behind us now, love. We mustn't linger on it."

He smiled at her. "You are quite right. We have a long, relaxing trip ahead of us that I can hardly wait to begin."

"You don't have to wait any longer, dear husband," she replied. "We have already begun."

Caroline Johnson

\*\*\*

## THE END

Visit us often at

**LoveLightFaith.com**

to learn about upcoming books and to read more about our authors.

## ABOUT THE AUTHOR

Caroline Johnson originally hails from the Midwest, but now enjoys the warmer temperatures and hospitality of the South. She is a firm believer that everybody deserves a happy ending. As a lover of romance, Caroline is passionate about touching other people's hearts with messages that true love always prevails.

Caroline's stories run the gamut of historical tales of love to modern romances with relatable heroes and heroines. Because of her strong faith, Caroline's stories are clean, wholesome and oftentimes Christian-based.

When she's not writing, Caroline is volunteering with her church or spending time with her husband, children and rescued pets. She loves hiking, biking, and exploring the beauty of nature, but is equally as fulfilled curled up on the couch with an almond milk latte and a good book.

Printed in Poland
by Amazon Fulfillment
Poland Sp. z o.o., Wrocław